KT-372-025

BAINTE DEN STOC

WITHDRAWN FROM
DÚN LAOGHAIRE-RATHDOWN COUNTY
LIBRARY STOCK

Dick Turpin:
Legends and Lies

by

Terry Deary

Illustrated by Zoografic

You do not need to read this page –
just get on with the book!

Published in 2007 in Great Britain by
Barrington Stoke Ltd
18 Walker St, Edinburgh, EH3 7LP

www.barringtonstoke.co.uk

Reprinted 2009

Copyright © 2007 Terry Deary
Illustrations © Zoografic

The moral right of the author has been asserted in
accordance with the Copyright, Designs and
Patents Act 1988

ISBN: 978-1-84299-456-6

Printed in Great Britain by Bell & Bain Ltd

Characters

James Smith,
the teacher

Dick Turpin

Mrs. Shelley

John Turpin,
the old man

The Boy

John Robinson,
the farmer

Contents

Chapter 1

The Crowd
Saturday 7th April 1739, York.

I remember the day Dick Turpin died.

Crowds filled the twisted streets of York City. They dressed in their best Sunday clothes and marched out of the city gates. They gathered in the fields outside the walls. They met at the scaffold where Turpin would die.

I got there early so I was near the front of the crowds. The scaffold was built of rough wood and I was pushed into a corner right beside it.

A stout woman in a green satin dress shook my arm. "You're too young to be here," she panted. I could tell from her voice that she wasn't from round here. She came from the south.

"You're never too young to watch a hanging," a farmer said. His hands were stained with the soil and his clothes smelled of cow muck and hay.

"My father said I had to come," I told the woman. "He said I had to watch Dick Turpin hang. It will teach me a lesson I'll never forget! Dad says I'll see what happens to villains!"

"Dick Turpin's not a villain!" an old man croaked. His voice was from the south as well. People had come from all over England to see this hanging.

A tall man, thin as a rope, gripped me by the ear. "Turpin was born a villain and he will die a villain." The tall man had glasses on the end of his nose and a worn black suit. "I taught him when he was a boy. I know."

The farmer, the woman, the old man and the teacher crowded into my corner for an hour. The last hour of Dick Turpin's life.

The Spring day was cool and showery. "You should be wearing a hat," the woman fussed. "It'll get warm before the day is done. You need the shade."

"I haven't got a hat," I said shyly. We were too poor for things like that. In the crowd she couldn't see my feet. I was too poor for shoes.

The woman shook her head. The farmer sneered. "I work all day in the sun. It does me no harm."

"It fried your brain," she snapped at him. She turned back to me. "If it gets too sunny you can stand in my shadow," she said.

That was kind. No one was ever kind to a boy like me. The woman had a soft face and white hands. "Is Dick Turpin really wicked?" I asked her.

"Of course not!" the farmer cut in. "He's a gentleman of the road!"

"You mean a thief!" the woman cried.

"A gentleman thief," the farmer told her.

"The boy should not be here," the woman went on. "To see a man die is a cruel thing. To see an evil man choke and go to Hell is not for a child."

"I'm not a child," I argued.

"How old are you?" she asked me. "Twelve?"

I shrugged. "I don't know."

The farmer spat. "You say the lad shouldn't be here. But you've come a long way to see Dick Turpin hang. *You're* here, lady. Why is that?"

"Revenge," she said softly. "Revenge."

Chapter 2
The Villain – Dick Turpin

The farmer leaned against the rail of the scaffold. He slid down so his face was level with mine. His teeth were yellow-green and his breath smelled of old onions. He wrapped a dirty hand around my shoulder. "Here, son, let me tell you about the time Dick Turpin robbed a robber!"

I just nodded.

"Dick Turpin was a poor lad, like you," the farmer said. "The rich folk don't care about us. They give us nothing. If we want money we have to work from dawn till dusk. We have to break our backs for pennies."

"Or steal it, like Turpin," I said.

The farmer nodded. "He was a poor butcher boy in London, you know?"

There were butcher shops in the Shambles – that was the name of a narrow street in York. They killed cattle at the back of the street and put the meat in the shops at the front. The smell of blood filled your head when you walked down there. "A dirty job," I said.

"Dick decided to make a little extra money," the farmer said. "He stole some sheep and cattle. He cut them up and sold the meat. He was only trying to make some money to live."

The teacher tapped the farmer on the shoulder. "Excuse me, but you look like a farmer."

The man squinted at him. "I am. Twenty cows and fifty sheep."

"You would not be happy if Turpin stole *your* animals," the teacher sniffed.

"That's different!" the farmer argued. "Now take your sharp and pointy nose and stick it in someone else's business! I was telling the lad about Turpin."

The teacher gave the farmer a hard stare and began to read a book. Don't ask me what it was. I never learned to read.

The farmer turned back to me. "Dick Turpin turned to highway robbery. He got himself a pistol and hid in the trees by the Radcliffe Highway. He didn't have to wait long before a stranger rode along. Turpin jumped out in front of him and waved the pistol. 'Stand and deliver!' he cried."

"Deliver what?" I asked.

The farmer frowned. "I don't know. Deliver his money, I guess. It's what highwaymen always say. Now, do you want to hear this story or not?"

"Yes, sir."

"Then shut up. Where was I?"

"Stand and deliver," I said.

"Ah yes ... stand and deliver. The man on the horse handed over a purse, then Turpin said, 'Give me that gold ring!' The

11

man on the horse said, 'It's my wedding ring. My wife will be upset if I lose it.'"

"Turpin wouldn't care," the lady in green satin muttered.

"But Turpin *did* care!" the farmer chuckled. "He asked what he could do and that's when his victim said, 'Fire your pistol at me!'"

"The man wanted Turpin to shoot him!" I gasped, and hopped from one freezing foot to the other.

The farmer smiled. "He wanted Turpin to put a bullet through his cloak. He wanted it to look as if he'd been in a fight and hadn't just handed over his wedding ring without a struggle."

"And did Turpin do it?" I asked.

"He did!"

"What happened then?"

"The man said, 'Now put a shot through my *hat*, please!' And Turpin said, 'I don't have a shot left in my pistol. I just fired it.' That's when the man drew a gun and pointed it at Turpin. 'Ah, but I have a shot in *my* pistol,' he said. 'I will shoot you if you don't hand me my purse and ring!'"

I laughed. "Turpin was tricked! Did the law get him?"

The farmer shook his head. "That's the best part of the story. It seems the man he'd stopped was Matthew King ... the famous highwayman!"

"Turpin tried to rob another highwayman?" I asked.

"He did. Of course, after that, the two men became great friends and the terrors of Epping Forest."

"Robbing the rich," I said. "Just like Robin Hood. He was a real hero, then."

The lady in the green satin dress grabbed my shoulder and shook me. "He was a villain," she said. "Don't believe the idiot tales. He was the most cruel man to ride the roads of Essex."

"He was a hero!" the farmer argued.

The woman leaned forward till her nose was close to his. "It is easy for you to say. You have just heard the stories. You don't know his victims."

The farmer spat. "Oh, and you do, eh?"

"I do."

"Who was that?" I asked.

"Me," she said. She spoke to me but kept her eyes on the farmer's face. "Turpin and his gang robbed *me*."

Chapter 3
The Victim – Mrs Shelley

The farmer pulled a face as if his green teeth were hurting. "Dick Turpin? Hurt a lady?"

The woman in green satin looked at him, as cold as the wind from the York moors. "Turpin is a bully. He was one of the Essex gang."

"I've heard of them," I said. "They broke into houses and robbed the owners."

The woman nodded. "There were at least six of them. They kicked down doors at lonely houses. They put pistols to the owners' heads. They made them show where their money was kept. They carried off everything they could and smashed the rest."

"That's spiteful," the farmer admitted.

"What did they do to you?" I asked.

The woman closed her eyes for a moment. "It was over four years ago. 1734. They broke down my front door and marched into my room. They all wore masks. They said they knew I had money hidden in the house. They said they would shoot me if I didn't tell."

"If they shot you then you would *never* be able to tell," the teacher said.

The woman gave a faint smile. "That's what I told them. So the leader of the gang – I think it was Turpin – went over to the kitchen fire and threw some logs on. He told his men to pick me up and carry me over to the fire."

"No!" I cried.

"They held me over the fire and the leader said he'd roast me alive if I didn't talk," the woman went on.

"So you talked," the teacher nodded.

"No! I did not! I said the gang could roast me if they wanted. It would be good for them to see it, I said. Because one day they will all roast in Hell!"

"Brave lady," the farmer said.

"Did they burn you?" I gasped.

The woman gave a sigh. "My son came to the house and he saw what they were doing. He told them where the money was. He thought he was saving his mother's life." She shook her head. "The men found a hundred pounds. They stayed to drink all my wine and roasted my meat."

"But you lived?" the teacher said.

"I lived in fear. I'm too afraid to ever sleep again. The shock and the horror haunts me."

"That's why you want revenge?" I asked. "That's why you want to see Turpin die?"

The woman nodded. "I want to sleep in peace. I saw the rest of the Essex gang hanged in London. Turpin is the last." She turned to the farmer. "*That's* the sort of man you called a hero, farmer."

The man shook his head. "Yes ... I mean, no. I was just telling you the stories that I heard about Turpin. There were other stories."

The teacher wagged a finger. "The story of Turpin killing Matthew King is a lesson to us all."

"Matthew King? Do you mean the highwayman he tried to rob? The man in the story you just told me? Did he become his enemy?" I asked.

The teacher pressed his thin lips into a hard smile. "Matthew King was his *friend*! Turpin shot his friend. What sort of a man does that?"

"It was an accident," the old man beside us muttered. But the teacher wasn't listening. He was looking inside his coat pocket. He pulled out a piece of newspaper.

"The real hero isn't Turpin," he said. "It was an inn-keeper who risked his life to arrest the highwayman Matthew King. The inn-keeper was called Richard Bayes. He tracked Turpin to London and caught him in a stable." The teacher took his glasses off and cleaned them. Then he read the newspaper to us.

"When Mr Bayes went to arrest King, then King drew out a pistol. He pressed it to Mr Bayes' chest and pulled the trigger. Luckily it didn't fire. King struggled to get out his other pistol but it was tangled in his pocket. Turpin was nearby, on horse-back, waiting for King. King cried out, 'Shoot him, Dick, or we will be caught, by God!' Turpin fired his pistol and it missed Mr Bayes. He shot King in two places and King cried out, 'Dick, you have killed me!' When Turpin heard that he rode away as fast as he could. King died a week later and told everyone Turpin was a coward."

The teacher folded the paper and put it back in his pocket.

The white-haired old man said, "Dick is no coward. Watch and see. He will die like a brave man."

The teacher patted his pocket and smirked. "A coward, sir. A coward," he said.

Chapter 4

The Fool – John Robinson, farmer

The farmer looked back up the road that came from York. "Not long now," he said.

The crowd was thicker. It pressed us forward onto the scaffold rails. I heard a soft rumble. It was like the distant roar of the River Ouse when it was flooding. It was the noise of the crowd cheering from a mile away down the road.

"It's Turpin," the teacher said, looking through his glasses and over the heads of the crowd. "Not long now."

The farmer looked at the woman. "You'll soon have your revenge then, lady."

"I wish I could push him off the ladder myself," she said.

The farmer rubbed a hand over his greasy hair and said, "In some ways I put Turpin there."

"Where?" I asked.

"I put him on the scaffold," he said. "He may be a great man but he's no match for John Robinson."

"John Robinson?" I asked. "Who's he?"

"Why, that's me, lad. I was the one that got Turpin arrested in York!"

"What did he do? Try to rob you?" I asked.

He shook his head. "Have you not heard the story? I'm as famous as Turpin!"

"You?" I said and rubbed my eyes.

"Turpin shot Matthew King and ran off to Yorkshire where no one knew him. He changed his name to John Palmer."

"We know that," the lady in the green dress said. "But I don't remember a story about John Robinson catching him."

"Then you should," the farmer said with a flash of anger. "Everybody in my village, Brough, knows me."

"We're not from your village," the teacher told him.

"I remember the day Dick Turpin rode past my farm," the farmer said. "He'd been drinking. I could tell. He was shouting and laughing with his friends."

"They'd been hunting," the old man with white hair said. "Harmless. A good day out. He was happy."

"His last happy day on earth," the teacher sneered.

"This is *my* story!" the farmer hissed. "Are you listening?"

"Yes, but be quick. I can see the cart with Turpin – he'll be here in a few minutes," the woman told him.

"Turpin rode through the village ... shouting and laughing ..."

"You said that already," the teacher snapped.

"And that was when he saw a cockerel – it belonged to Francis Hall, the cow-man. The cockerel screamed at Turpin and he stopped laughing. He pulled out his pistol, walked over to the gate and shot it. I remember it well."

"So you said."

"Was that when you caught him?" I asked.

"No ... you don't go catching a man with a pistol, son. But I told him he'd have to pay for it. 'I saw you shoot that poor bird!' I told him. And you won't believe what he said to me ..." The farmer waited a moment.

"But you're going to tell us," the teacher said.

"'Wait until I load my pistol, and I'll shoot you too!' That's what Turpin said."

"Was *that* when you caught him?" I asked.

"Not exactly. I went to the law officer and reported what I'd seen. I told them John Palmer had killed Hall's cockerel and *then* said he'd kill me!"

"So you didn't really catch Dick Turpin, did you?" I asked.

"I was the man that had Dick Turpin arrested. I should have the £200 reward."

The teacher shook his head slowly. "No, my friend. You did *not* have Dick Turpin arrested."

"I did – I tell you, I did!"

"No. You had *John Palmer* arrested," the teacher said, and wagged his thin finger again.

"It's the same man. Dick Turpin *was* John Palmer," the farmer argued.

"Ah, but nobody *knew* that. Palmer was arrested. He would have paid a fine and then gone free. No, my farmer friend, the real hero in Turpin's tale is *me!*"

Chapter 5

The Traitor – James Smith, teacher

The teacher took off his glasses and polished them on the sleeve of his worn black coat.

"I should have the reward, you know. Turpin had a price of £200 on his head. And they only caught Turpin because of me."

The old man looked at him, and his eyes were filled with hate. "Traitor," he muttered.

The teacher sniffed and turned his back on the old man. He looked at the lady in green satin and said, "Everyone in York thought Turpin was the horse thief, John Palmer. He was safe!"

"A horse thief could hang, of course," the lady said.

"Ah!" The teacher nodded and waved a thin white finger. "But if they knew he was really Dick Turpin, then he would be hanged for sure. Oh, yes, I should have the reward."

"What did you do?" I asked. I shuffled my bare feet on the cobbles. They were cold.

The teacher looked at me as if I were a sour smell. His eyes were huge and round behind the glasses. "When he was in prison in York, Turpin wrote a letter to his sister. He sent the letter from York prison all the way home to Hempstead in Essex. He wanted her husband to raise some money and set him free. But her husband refused to pay the postage on the letter!"

I nodded. No one ever sent my family letters. We were happy about that. If someone sends you a letter you have to pay for it. We never had enough money. "So did *you* pay for Turpin's letter?" I asked.

"No. But I knew who'd *sent* it! I knew that hand-writing. I taught Turpin how to write twenty years ago."

The teacher's face had pink spots in his winter cheeks now. He turned back to the woman. "I knew it was a letter from Turpin – the most wanted man in England. I took it straight to the law officer. Oh, yes, upon my soul, I told him, 'That's the writing of Dick Turpin the highway robber.'"

The woman said, "And murderer, don't forget. He was wanted for murder too."

The teacher wasn't listening. His gooseberry eyes were glowing. "They sent me all the way up here to York. They showed me the prisoners in the jail and I knew him at once. I pointed him out." The teacher stretched out an arm – in his mind he was back in the prison. "'That's Turpin,' I said."

"And it was," the woman said with a sigh.

"Of course, at first Turpin tried to say I was a liar. He said he'd never seen me. They found other people to say it was Turpin. But I was the first. Upon my soul, the very first."

"Traitor," the old man snarled. "Giving away an old friend from school. What sort of gutter rat would do that?"

The woman in green frowned. "He was doing his duty."

"My duty," the teacher agreed.

"You'll be happy to see him hang ... you gutter rat," the old man said.

"We *all* will," the woman said.

"*I* won't!" the man told her angrily.

"So? Why are you here?" she snapped back.

"To see a man die. A real man."

Chapter 6

The Man – John Turpin, inn-keeper

The crowd roared and cheered as Turpin came in sight. Turpin nodded back bravely. "He looks pale," the woman said. "That's fear."

The old man with white hair turned on her. "He has been locked in York Castle for months. He hasn't seen the sun in all that time."

And the sun was shining weakly through the cold, thin April clouds. The teacher sniffed, "I hope he enjoys it. It's the last sun he'll ever see!"

Turpin's hands were tied. The guards helped him get down from the cart. They looked more afraid than Turpin. Five men in black suits watched silently. "They are the mourners," the farmer said.

"Are they Turpin's friends?" I asked.

The teacher sneered. "No. Turpin paid them to be here. They will guard his body."

"Guard it?"

"Oh, yes." The teacher nodded wisely. "The doctors will want to claim the corpse once Turpin is dead. They will cut it up and show their students how the human body works."

"That would be a sin and a crime," the old man moaned. "The mourners will see the lad safe under ground."

Turpin wore a rich new coat. "They say hundreds of people went to see him in prison," I said. "They gave him gifts, money and wine."

The farmer nodded. "He'll die a rich man!"

Turpin walked from the cart to the scaffold and passed us so close we could touch him. The old man stretched out a hand and clutched the highwayman's sleeve. "Bless you, son!" he called.

The guards shoved the hand away and pushed Turpin towards the ladder. Turpin turned and called back to the old man, "It's a fine day to die, Father!"

The woman tried to move away from the old man but the crowd was pressing too hard. "You are that villain's father?"

The old man nodded and raised his chin with pride. He looked down at me and rubbed my hair. "I remember Dick when he was a lad like this. You see a thief and an outlaw. I just see my little boy."

"He was always a cruel bully in school," the teacher said.

The old man spat, "You taught him badly. And when he was caught it was *you* that betrayed him. I wish it was you up on the scaffold and not my son."

The teacher had no answer.

Turpin was shown the ladder and he placed a foot on the bottom rung. His leg was shaking. He stamped the foot on the platform to steady it and the crowd cheered. "Say something!" a voice cried out.

Turpin turned and waited till a man in a black mask put a noose over his head. He climbed a few more steps. The crowd went silent. Turpin wasn't a handsome man. His face was marked by scars of the smallpox disease.

"I never meant to harm anyone," he called out.

The woman in the green satin dress gave a snort of disgust.

"I only tried to make a living," Turpin shouted. "I wasn't born rich. I had to make my own way in life. I did the best I could. And now I go to a better place!"

"I hope you go to Hell," the woman muttered.

The crowd had just begun to cheer the bold words when Turpin threw himself off the ladder. I didn't see him die. I turned my head away.

The woman took my head and buried my face in the soft satin of her dress. I heard the muttering voices. The woman turned to the farmer. "You were wrong. You told the boy that you're never too young to watch a hanging," she said.

I looked up but kept my eyes turned away from the scaffold. The old man's face was cold as iron. "They say revenge tastes sweet," he said softly. "Does it taste sweet to see my son die?"

The woman shook her head slowly. "It tastes bitter. So bitter."

The old man turned to the teacher. "And how does it feel to betray a man?" he asked.

"I was doing my duty," the teacher said.

"You taught my boy to read. He was the same age as this lad here," he said and touched my shoulder.

"Turpin gave me a lot of trouble in school."

"Ah, so you betrayed him out of spite," the old man went on.

The farmer growled, "That's nasty, that is. A teacher should be kinder than that."

"And you?" the old man said. "You came to see a man die. You're no better." He turned and walked away from us.

The body of Turpin was being loaded onto the cart and the crowd was drifting away. The old man waited for it to pass and began to walk behind it.

"Where are you going?" the woman asked suddenly.

"To the Blue Boar Inn," old Mr Turpin said. "My son will be laid out at the inn before his funeral tomorrow." He swayed a little as the cart with the body rolled past. I thought he was going to faint away.

"Take my arm, Mr Turpin," the woman said.

He nodded, silently. The two enemies walked off arm in arm.

The farmer rubbed his rough hands and gave the teacher a nudge. "That's not the end of Turpin. You'll see. That's not the end."

Chapter 7

The Body –
Doctor Marmaduke Palms

I didn't sleep. I lay shivering in the straw and listened to the rats in the darkness. Every time I closed my eyes I saw Turpin jumping off the ladder.

The stories of Turpin raced around York. My father came home that night panting to tell the tale he'd heard.

"Do you know how Turpin escaped the law?"

"He shot his friend Matthew King and rode off to hide," I said.

"The story I heard was, he did a robbery in London. He was spotted. So he jumped on his mighty mare – a horse they called Black Bess. He rode like the wind and not even the wind could catch him. He was in York the next evening and he rode up to the Mayor of York! The Mayor! Imagine that!"

"But why would he do that?" I asked.

"When people said Turpin had robbed someone in London he went to the Mayor. The Mayor said it could not have been Turpin! How could Turpin be in London one day and York the next? The Mayor of York said no one could ride that fast!"

"I've never heard of this Black Bess," I said.

"No, she dropped down dead at the end of the ride. But Turpin lived on. Oh, yes." Then my father said what the farmer had said. "You haven't heard the last of Turpin."

But the next night my father had another tale. As I lay in my straw I heard my father whisper to my mother, "They say the body-snatcher will have Turpin before the night is done!"

I didn't know what a body-snatcher was. But the name made me shiver too much for sleep. I got up from my bed and put a sack round my shoulders. I wandered into York to see the grave where Turpin lay.

It was in St George's churchyard. I had to see for myself. If Turpin was at rest, I thought, maybe *I* could get some rest.

I peered over the churchyard wall and froze. There was some pale yellow light above one of the graves. At first I thought it was a spirit rising from the ground. Then I heard the soft scrape of wooden spades.

The yellow light was a lantern and the spades were the tools of the body-snatchers.

I watched as they dragged the coffin out of the soil and quickly filled in the hole.

There were four men. They placed their spades on the coffin and raised it onto their shoulders. They walked to the gate and turned towards me. The man at the front held the lantern up to my face.

Suddenly he laughed. "I told you, boy. I told you it wasn't the end of Turpin!" In the pale glow I saw the dirty face of the farmer who had stood at the scaffold. I smelled his farmyard smell.

"Where are you taking him?" I asked.

"To the surgeon. To Doctor Marmaduke Palms – he'll pay us well," the farmer said.

The men set off down the dark streets. I followed. I had that idea in my head, I would never sleep in peace again till Turpin did.

I saw the men take the coffin to a small garden of a house on the edge of town, and lay it in a shallow new grave. They went to the door and vanished inside.

I turned and ran. Cobbles stung my bare feet and I slid over gutter mud and horse droppings. At last I reached the Blue Boar Inn and hammered on the door. A window opened. "Who's there?" someone shouted out.

"I want to see Mr Turpin!" I cried.

"He's not here any more. They hanged him yesterday and buried him this morning. Go away."

"They hanged Dick Turpin's father?" I gasped.

"No. They hanged Dick Turpin. The body was brought here but they took it and buried it again this morning," the person shouted back.

"I know ... but someone just dug him up and took him to the doctor for cutting up."

"They can't do that!"

"I know ... I want you to tell old Mr Turpin – see if he can do something!"

"We'll do something, son. Wait there!"

The window closed. Lights flared in the inn and I could hear angry voices.

The rest of that night is as much a dream as my nightmare of when Turpin jumped off the ladder at the scaffold. A crowd of men and women carried flaming torches down the twisting streets. They followed me in a grim line as I led them to the doctor's gate.

The men at the front of the line pushed open the doctor's gate and began to scrape away the earth on the shallow grave. The doctor poked his weasel head out of a window. "Who's there?"

"We've come for young Turpin, you foul monster. We're taking him back to his proper grave," the inn-keeper roared.

"If you try to stop us you might end up in the same grave!" old Mr Turpin put in. The other men cheered him.

"Oh, no!" the doctor croaked. "I never wanted the body anyway! Take it and good luck to you. It's not my fault. Let Turpin rest in peace!" He slammed the window shutter and we heard bolts slide into place.

The line of people that went back to St George's churchyard was quieter now. Dick

Turpin was laid to rest a third and final time.

I made my way slowly back to the Blue Boar Inn with old Mr Turpin resting on my shoulder.

He stopped at the door and turned. He wrapped his arms around me. "You did well, boy. You did well. You have a good heart. My Dick would have done the same."

"Thank you, sir."

"Don't end up like him," he said, and his voice was breaking.

"No, sir."

"We can all rest now," he whispered.

I felt the old man's warm tears falling on my head.

Epilogue –
Legends and lies

The boy's story is made up. But the people he met in the story were real enough.

The stories of the body snatch and the rescue are true too. Doctor Palms was arrested.

Dick's grave can still be seen in York.

Dick was held in York Castle and you can visit his cell in the Castle Museum.

And Turpin's tale was true. He really did shoot his partner, Matthew King.

He did escape the law in London. He did make a stupid mistake and get arrested for shooting a cockerel. Truth.

He was betrayed by his teacher. Truth.

But people need heroes. Over the years people began to add to Turpin's story. They invented a wonderful horse for him called Black Bess. A lie.

They added a story that Turpin rode from London to York in a day to escape the law. Brave Bess dropped dead at the end. Lies.

Films and books have made Dick Turpin look like a gentleman. Lies.

He was a cruel bully. Truth.

He died well ... but he lived badly. Truth.

Barrington Stoke would like to thank all its readers for commenting on the manuscript before publication and in particular:

Carla Aiton
Callum Baines
Joe Bodin
Blair Campbell
Alex Chisholm
Cynthia Clift
Sam Davis
Kelly Dawson
Demi Dunlop
Lindsay Gomm
Jordan King
Mary Anne Kruger
CJ Maxtone
Kasia McCandless
Carl McElroy
Judith McIntyre
James Moran
Christina Nicholls
Patrick Anthony Nicholson

Joshua Nugent
Craig O'Connor
Aseef Rashid
Callum Robertson
Aqib Saleem
Daniel Saville-Searles
Carla Seaborne
Chloe Seaborne
Alfie-Rae Smith
Stephen Smith
Emma Simpson
Jordan Tapp
Belle Terry
Malisa Testa
Kristina Wardlaw
Charlie Willis
Evie Wise
Mrs Woodward
Jade Wright

Become a Consultant!

Would you like to give us feedback on our titles before they are published? Contact us at the e-mail address below – we'd love to hear from you!

info@barringtonstoke.co.uk
www.barringtonstoke.co.uk

WANTED

Terry Deary

Favourite villain:

Mary Ann Cotton (1830–1873). Mary killed about 15 of her own children and 3 husbands. She fed the children with arsenic poison from a teapot. They died a slow and painful death. Mary was arrested and hanged.

Favourite hero:

Guy Fawkes. The evil Tudors and Stuarts were killing and torturing his friends, the Catholics. He risked his own life to end their suffering. Sadly he was caught and suffered awful tortures bravely. In the end they executed him. The torturers' names are forgotten but Guy's name still lives on.

What would your name be if you were an outlaw?

Terry the Terrible – member of the School Scraggers gang. "Rob the rich, pay the poor – rob the teachers to pay the pupils!"

If you were going to be hung, what would your last words to the crowd be?

Deary me!

WANTED

Zoografic

Favourite villain:

Belmonte: Long John Silver.
Chris: Olrik.

Favourite hero:

Belmonte: Cortos Maltes (a comic book adventurer/sailor).
Chris: Tintin.

What period of history would you like to live in? And why?

Chris: I like living now. I think the clothes are really nice now – especially the women's clothes!

Belmonte: I wish I'd lived in Paris, at the end of the 19th century. There were so many great artists then, doing amazing things. I would like to live in the studio of one of the great artists of the time – to see if I could learn something!

If you were going to be hung, what would your last words to the crowd be?

Belmonte: I would say nothing.
Chris: Please can I go to the toilet?

Try another book in the
REALITY CHECK
series

Also out now ...

Pocket Hero

by Pippa Goodhart

The amazing true story of Jeffrey Hudson.
Jeffrey was a human pet, a slave, a Captain
in the army, killed a man in a duel and was
captured by pirates. And he was only
45 cm tall!

The Land of Whizzing Arrows

by Simon Chapman

Terrifying true story of explorer
Leo Parcus. Jungles and jaguars, crocodiles
and cannibals. Watch out – this book bites!

Also by the same author ...

The Last Viking

Emma has heard that the Vikings cut the throats of the old and carry away their young to be their slaves. So when she sees their ships coming she knows she must warn her village before it's too late. But will they believe her? Will she be able to save them all in time?

All available from our website:
www.barringtonstoke.co.uk